Baby's bedtime

Fiona Watt

pictures by Rachel Wells

managing designer: Mary Cartwright   series

D1510744

First published in 1999, Usborne Publishing Ltd, Usborne House, 83–85 Saffron Hill, London, EC1N 8RT. www.usborne.com © 1999 Usborne Publishing Ltd.
The name Usborne and the device ⊕ are Trademarks of Usborne Publishing Ltd. All rights reserved. No part of this publication may be reproduced,
stored in a retrieval system or transmitted in any form or by any means, electronic, mechanical, photocopying, recording, or otherwise, without
previous permission of the publisher. First published in America 1999. Printed in Belgium.

I'm ready for bed.

We look at some books...

...while I have my drink.

Upstairs to bed. Come on Fido.

Where's Bunny gone?

I always take Bunny to bed.

We want a goodnight kiss.

Put the night light on.
Close the curtains.

Are you tired, Bunny?

I'm getting sleepy.

Night, night Fido. Sleep tight.